PEACE WEEK
in Miss Fox's Class

Eileen Spinelli

Illustrated by Anne Kennedy

Albert Whitman & Company, Morton Grove, Illinois

Library of Congress Cataloging-in-Publication Data

Spinelli, Eileen.
Peace Week in Miss Fox's Class / by Eileen Spinelli ; illustrated by Anne Kennedy.
p. cm.
Summary: For "Peace Week," the animals in Miss Fox's class find ways to be peaceful instead of squabbling
with each other.
ISBN 978-0-8075-6379-3
[1. Conduct of life—Fiction. 2. Schools—Fiction. 3. Animals—Fiction.] I. Kennedy, Anne, 1955- ill. II. Title.
PZ7.S7566Pe 2009 [E]—dc22 2008031038

The illustrations were done in watercolors, ink, and dyes.
The design is by Carol Gildar.

For more information about Albert Whitman & Company,
please visit our web site at www.albertwhitman.com.

To the Chautauqua Institution,
a peaceable kingdom.—E.S.

For Mrs. LaRoche and Mrs. Berglund,
my favorite teachers.—A.K.

The children in Miss Fox's class had been squabbling. And squabbling. Day after day.

"Okay, that does it!" said Miss Fox. "We're having Peace Week."

Mouse piped up. "What's Peace Week, Miss Fox?"

"For one thing," replied Miss Fox, "no more squabbling. For one whole week."

Frog said, "What else, Miss Fox?"

Miss Fox sat on the edge of her desk. "It's your Peace Week. You design it. Any ideas, children?"

"No fighting!" called Bunny.

"Don't say mean things!" said Raccoon.

"Help others!" said Squirrel.

"Very good, children," said Miss Fox. "I think you have the idea. Let Peace Week begin!"

That afternoon, Squirrel's big sister yelled at Squirrel. "Stop bouncing nuts against the gate. You're giving me a headache."

Squirrel wanted to yell back. He wanted to say, "You are not the big old boss of me!"

But this was Peace Week.
So Squirrel bounced marshmallows instead.

On Tuesday, Bunny wore her yellow sweater to school.
Polecat poked fun at Bunny. "Here comes Bunny-Banana,"
he teased.

Bunny wanted to poke fun at Polecat's green sweater.
She wanted to say, "Here comes Pickle-puss."
But this was Peace Week.

So Bunny said, "My yellow sweater is cozy-warm,
Polecat. Your green sweater looks cozy-warm, too."

On Wednesday, Mouse went to the playground.
A bunch of little mice were quarreling in the sandbox.
"That's my shovel!" "That's my bucket!"

Mouse wanted to scamper right past them. She wanted to swing on the monkey bars and have her own fun.

But this was Peace Week.

So Mouse stopped. She sat in the sandbox with the little mice.

She showed them that if they worked together they could make a bigger and better sand castle.

On Thursday, Frog's Frisbee
bounced into Mr. Turtle's flowerbed.
Mr. Turtle scolded Frog.
Frog sighed. Mr. Turtle was
such a grump.
But this was Peace Week.

So Frog apologized.

Then Frog said, "By the way, Mr. Turtle, my mom thinks you have the prettiest garden in the neighborhood."

Mr. Turtle looked so shocked that Frog thought he was about to get scolded again.

But Mr. Turtle said, "I'm glad somebody noticed."

He smiled as he clipped the loveliest rose on the bush. "Give this to your mother," he said. "And don't forget your Frisbee."

On Friday morning, Mama Bear said, "Who will fetch the honey for our toast?"

Young Bear was busy making a paper airplane. He told his sister, "It's your turn."

Sister Bear was busy cleaning out her backpack. She said, "Yesterday was my turn. It's your turn today."

"Aha!" said Young Bear. "You did not fetch the honey yesterday. Yesterday we had bread and jam."
Sister Bear sniffed. "So?"
"So it's your turn today."
"Is not!"
"Is too!"

Suddenly Young Bear remembered—this was Peace Week.
He said, "Let's make a chart! That way we'll be able to keep
track of who fetches the honey."

  Sister Bear nodded.
"OK with me. But who will
fetch the honey now?"
  "I will," said Young Bear. "As soon as
I test-fly my paper airplane."
  Sister Bear said, "No, let me do it.
My backpack is clean now."

On Saturday, Raccoon went
to watch her favorite soccer team,
the Rinky-Dinks. She wore her gray and pink jersey.
    Possum was there, too. Possum was wearing her blue
jersey. Possum was cheering for the Blue Comets.
    Every time the Blue Comets made a goal, Possum
would pinch her nose, turn to Raccoon, and chant:

"Gray and pink! Rinky-Dinks stink!"

And so when the Rinky Dinks won the game, Raccoon made up her own chant:

"Wow! Blue Comets.
Ow! Blue Comets.
Who is stinky now?
Blue Comets!"

But Raccoon kept it in her head and didn't say it because this was Peace Week. Instead, Raccoon patted Possum on the back and said, "Good game!"

Possum gave Raccoon a little smile. "Maybe we can sit together at the next game."

On Monday, Miss Fox heard all about Peace Week.

"I was nice to little mice," said Mouse.

"I worked things out with my sister," said Bear.

"I made Mr. Turtle smile," said Frog.

Miss Fox beamed. "Good job, children. I say we celebrate!"

Miss Fox reached into her big bags. Out came streamers and balloons. Out came oatmeal cookies and apple slices.

"I like Peace Week," said Mouse.

"Me, too," said Bunny.

"I have a great idea!" Squirrel grinned. "Let's make every week Peace Week!"

And so they did.